THE SULTAN OF GARBAGE

THE SULTAN OF GARBAGE

BRIAN BELEFANT

atmosphere press

Published by Atmosphere Press

Cover design by Matthew Fielder

Atmospherepress.com

DEDICATION

I'm in a book club. Every month we get together to have a beer or two, catch up about what's going on with our lives, and discuss a book we've read.

One month, the book we were discussing was The Metamorphosis *by Franz Kafka.*

I hated it.

I hated the premise, hated the writing, hated the characters, hated the story, hated the inconsistencies. I hated everything about that book.

But then this new guy, Sasha, said six words that utterly transformed my understanding of The Metamorphosis. *With six words, Sasha not only made the book make sense, but made me realize the magnitude of Kafka's genius, for not just having written the story, but for having written the story the way he did.*

This book is dedicated to Sasha. I hope somewhere out there, there's a Sasha for it.

May every writer's book find its Sasha.

I'M LOOKING OUT at this island, stretching toward the horizon and rising into the sky, a blight on the relentless blue that surrounds it, water below, sky above, and it almost feels alive, like it's been waiting for me. I've never seen it before, but I know this place. And it knows me. I take it all in, as much as I can, and I say to myself, "I'm going to make this mine."

"Of course you are," she says from somewhere behind me.

Guess I'd said it out loud. I do that sometimes, say things out loud when I think I'm thinking to myself.

Her voice sounds weary when she says that. Like me saying how I might want to do something by myself, for myself, like that's some kind of an imposition.

I should back up. My name is Alex. Hers is Grace. And before we found ourselves on a sixty-foot yacht, thousands of miles from the nearest continent, in the middle of the Pacific Ocean, we were sitting in the living room of our condo, my condo. She was sitting. I'd just come in from taking out the trash and wondering why someone with a net worth of just under $4 million was still taking out the trash.

I sat down next to her but not touching—she doesn't like

uninvited touching—and apparently I said that out loud, too.

"You could hire someone to take care of it," she said, in this distracted way she has, more interested in the drama unfolding on the reality show on TV than in whatever was bothering me. And for good reason. When you think about it, they spend a lot of money to make reality shows interesting. Nobody spends money to make you interesting.

"Or I could ask you to help," I thought. I was careful not to say that out loud. God knows what would have happened if I'd actually said those words. Besides, she was wearing her slippers, the velvet ones from that little shop on the Rue Marguerite. The ones she'd fawned over when we took that spur-of-the-moment trip to Paris to celebrate, sort of, the sale of the studio, but which I put my foot down about buying because seriously? Who pays 640 euros for a pair of slippers?

But then the rest of the trip was kind of... off. I could feel—not quite resentment, but disappointment. We ate dinner at l'Ami Louis in silence, even though Evan and Nadine had made her promise we'd go there because the roast chicken there was the best in the world. At the Louvre, I slipped 100 euros to the woman in the kiosk and got us into the museum ahead of the entire line, but even that barely raised an eyebrow.

So two weeks before her birthday, I tracked down the phone number of the little shop and not that she asked, but under the pretext of having to prepare for an assignment I was being considered for, snuck out of the condo at four in the morning and called. I managed to speak with the saleslady who'd helped us. Yes, of course she remembered madame, she told me. Madame. Madame is what you call a woman over thirty, and Grace wasn't thirty, not for another two weeks, and any good salesperson would know better than to assume. I should have hung up right then, but I had no idea where else to get those slippers.

Yes, they still had the slippers, the very ones madame had been so delighted with. Yes, they could arrange to have them shipped to the US, but of course it might involve some considerable expense.

I paid, for the slippers as well as for the considerable expense, with the Visa card I was supposed to use for business expenses, the one that had the bills sent directly to Kathryn, the business manager Tony set me up with, and now that the studio was gone, I had to figure out where to have the package shipped. I arranged to have it shipped to Dan, who lives around the corner. I could trust Dan.

The birthday gift was a success. She was impressed, grateful. She'd even invited my touch when we'd gone to bed that night, which, I'll be honest, doesn't happen as much as I'd like it to anymore.

Since then she wore the slippers every day, all day, unless she had to go to an audition or, more likely, "jet out to meet a friend for coffee."

Anyway. She was sitting on the couch in her slippers, and I'd just come in from taking out the trash and was wondering why a person with a net worth of just under $4 million still had to take out the trash, and rather than offering to help, she suggested that I might hire somebody to take care of it and my mind went somewhere else completely.

I thought about trash.

"Why do people have so much trash?" I thought to myself.

"Why do you have so much trash?" I answered. I've had conversations with myself as long as I can remember, most of them, I hope, in my head.

"Because it won't fit into their home."

"That's stupid. It won't fit into a trash can, either. And the trash can is smaller."

"Slightly."

"Not the point."

"So what is the point?"

"The point is that we generate too much trash."

"We all do."

"That's what I'm saying. And where does all this trash end up? It goes into a trash can and gets taken away, with all the trash from all the trash cans and dumpsters, every goddamn week."

I looked over, checking to see if I'd actually said any of the two-sided conversation out loud. Judging by the way she was paying attention to the show, either I hadn't, or if I had, she didn't notice.

"I'm going to bed," she declared, clicking off the TV and putting the remote down on the coffee table. "I have a splitting headache."

It's sad. She gets these splitting headaches just about every night. Or a backache.

"Okay, I'm going to stay up and get some work done," I answered. When she's not feeling okay, my touch is definitely not invited.

And that's how it started. I got up and poured myself a glass of bourbon, then grabbed my laptop and sat on Ernie the chair, back against one arm and legs over the other, the way I always sit on Ernie the chair. I wanted Ernie the chair to be comfortable—he looked comfortable, but he never really was. This is the only way I can stand sitting in him.

I can't tell you how many hours I sat in Ernie the chair, perusing the internet, finding out where all the trash ends up, which believe me was a lot less annoying than clicking on call for entries and rearranging my portfolio and revising cover letters. Did you know that the Getty Museum was built on top of a huge landfill? There's something satisfying about that, about how the museum had never accepted any of my work into its photography collection, but some of it might actually be there anyway, buried underneath it, among used hypodermic needles and take-out containers and soda bottles.

And then I found out about the massive island of garbage floating out in the middle of the Pacific. I became overcome with this desire, this need, to see it. And why not? I had plenty of money and not a single assignment on the horizon. What would it cost to hire a boat and go out there, to the middle of the ocean, and put my eyes on it? Out where there wouldn't be LinkedIn or job postings or even assignments to shoot photos for ads hawking crap nobody needs for money they don't have.

MY EYES SNAP OPEN to the call of a fucking annoying bird right outside the bedroom window. The stupid alarm hasn't even gone off yet. It happens every goddamn morning, earlier and earlier as the days get longer. Some people find the singing of birds delightful. I think they're pathetic. They're mating calls. Advertisements. Broadcasting to the entire neighborhood, "Look at me! I'm hot! Buy me!"

I'm in a mood. Out of sorts. Again. This happens pretty much every morning when I wake up anymore, like I'd been fighting my way through a bad dream. Not a nightmare, really, but a dream that made me uneasy. Like there's something I should be dealing with, but I'm not.

Whatever.

The songbirds go off at dawn, but after a while the crows come on, with their drama, bitching about a hawk or a neighborhood cat or letting each other in on some new place to eat—a garbage can that got knocked over or a squirrel dead in the road. The crows take breaks every once in a while, like the way a reality show cuts to a commercial break, and the songbirds go at it again. I argue amongst myself about this all the time, but can't come to an agreement about which I like less. Sure, the songbirds are more pleasing to the ear—better production values, bigger budgets—but the crows get points for gritty authenticity, even if their braying is grating.

People like to say that there aren't seasons in LA, but if you live here long enough, you get to realize that there actually are. Not snow, flowers, hot, and crisp—the seasons they show in the movies, the seasons of America—but rainy with occasional hot-and-windy, clear with the scent of jasmine, gloomy skies offset by purple jacaranda, and hot. Funny how the place that makes movies makes movies with seasons that are entirely different from the seasons in the place where the movies are actually being made.

It's spring, and spring in LA comes with glare. The sun pops up hot and bright, hotter and brighter than during the rest of the year, maybe because there's less smog—all those agents and managers and actors and directors off on ski vacations and film festivals, their sports cars and SUVs not vomiting exhaust into the air. Whatever the reason, the light comes blasting through the east-facing windows earlier and earlier, ricocheting off of every surface and waking my lazy ass long before I want to be out of bed and starting my day.

The glare through the window this morning is super intense, making me want to close my eyes again, to shut it out, but the light is too bright. I hate the light. I hate the light, but I'm a fucking photographer. I can't live without it.

Grace is amazing. The light never seems to bother her. She can sleep through anything—not just the light and the fucking bird songs and the constant shhhhhh, shhhhhh, shhhhhh of the traffic on the 405 two blocks away, but even car alarms, Angela the slutty neighbor downstairs having sex with a different man every night, loud and proud, like she's showing off, like she's starring in her own porno movie, and the Bap-Bap! of car tires on the loose manhole cover which for some reason drivers seem to aim at just as I'm dropping off to sleep, and the rev of Dan's motorcycle, every night at midnight when he starts it up to head out to the bars to troll for the fat chicks visiting from Iowa he has a thing for. She sleeps through clouds of acrid cigarette smoke that waft over from Amir's place, a six-foot high fence not high enough to keep it from rolling in on the still air into the condo even when all the windows are closed and the air conditioning is on. She sleeps through the police helicopters—oh, those goddamn police helicopters!—patrolling the neighborhood just about every night, piercing the darkness with their spotlights, setting off chain reactions of barking dogs. And yeah, she sleeps through the mating calls of the fucking birds. Especially the mating calls.

I heave myself out of bed, wander into the bathroom, and pee. Then I snatch up a cup I keep in the bathroom, fill it with water, and bring it back into the living room to pour onto the roots of this little tree by the window. Watering the toilet and the ficus, I like to think of it. Back into the bathroom, where I put down the cup and take a shower.

Then coffee.

When Tony told me he'd decided to sell the studio—and that I'd come into some money as a result—I thought about buying myself an espresso machine. Not just any espresso machine, but an Elektra Microcasa Semiautomatica, the most beautiful espresso machine ever made, all copper and brass, with elegant little pipes and a golden eagle, wings spread like it's coming in for a landing on the domed top. I first saw one in a pasticceria in San Gimignano, a place that felt like it was stuck in a time warp, like when you walked through the door you were suddenly in black and white, like it was 1953. The machine is stupid expensive, and I actually came this close to ordering one.

But then I found il orfano.

Il orfano was free, discarded, among a neat pile of stuff along the curb that had been left for someone—me—to collect, like maybe somebody had renounced all their worldly possessions and moved into an ashram. Or maybe got sent to prison.

Or maybe died, and whoever was responsible for cleaning out their things never heard about Goodwill.

I didn't see il orfano at first. My eyes went straight to an old end table with an inlaid top and intricately carved legs, but the damn thing was too heavy to carry, so I took inventory of the other items available. Hiding behind a tidy stack of dress shirts, not my size, there it was, almost like it was cowering. The poor thing was old, brown, and beat up. Its cord was frayed.

I took the espresso machine home, thinking I'd come back in the car for the end table, but of course I had to plug it in and see if it worked, and it did. It made a pretty crappy espresso, but I found out with a lot of practice that I could make a better one if I ground the beans just right and tamped them into the thing hard, but not too hard. So it probably took me like twenty minutes to get back, and by the time I did, the end table had been smashed. It looked like somebody had taken a sledgehammer to it. The clothes, too, were scattered and torn. The whole thing made me sad, and that's why I took to calling the espresso machine 'il orfano'—the orphan, in Italian—at least to myself.

I knew, of course, that the espresso machine was female. Not just because of the way it (she) looked, sleek and sexy, but also its (her) name: La Pavoni. Said so right there on the front of the base, in that circular metal signet with the mid-century modern type and the adorable crown. The model was a Europiccola, also feminine, but "la orfana" doesn't roll off the tongue the way "il orfano" does, and besides, maybe she (it) identifies as a he.

Maybe, but who was I to presume, I asked myself.

I saw my point. But I decided to ignore what I told myself. I do that a lot.

When I got back home after seeing the smashed up end table, Grace was in the kitchen, staring at il orfano. "What's that?" she asked.

"My new coffee maker," I told her.

"New?"

"New to me."

She smiled, but I could tell she was disappointed. She'd been talking about getting a better coffee maker, one that would make her life easier, and this—il orfano—was definitely not that, so I went over to Best Buy and bought her one of those fancy Keurig coffee makers, along with a chrome rack to hold the array of plastic single-use coffee pods she could choose from. She loves that Keurig coffee maker. She tells me just about every time she makes a cup how good it is. Sometimes she'll even make one for me, and yeah, they are good. But there's something special about il orfano. It's one of the two things Grace can't get me to let go of, the other being the ficus. My realtor gave it to me when I bought the condo, and I was determined, obligated, to keep it alive.

Okay, three things. There's Ernie the chair.

Ernie the chair is an armchair that I came across at a garage sale. I was walking by, talking to myself, and when I saw the thing—a big, overstuffed beast with gashes where some cat had used it as a scratching post—I kind of just blurted out, "What an awesome chair!"

The woman running the garage sale heard me and called from over by the kitchen stuff, "Oh, that's Ernie." That's what I heard, anyway. In retrospect, she'd probably said, "Oh, that's Ernie's." She came over and appraised the chair with me, like she was thinking of buying it herself. "Shame he had to go off to prison," she said, probably talking about Ernie the person and not Ernie the chair.

"How much do you want for him?" I asked, meaning the chair and not the person.

"Fifteen bucks."

You couldn't beat fifteen bucks for a chair like that, so I bought it. I had to carry it the seven blocks to my condo, upside down on my head, thankful that the seat cushion didn't smell like urine and was well-stuffed because the weight of it compressed my spine, and placed it in the living room where it looked... like shit. But about a month later, I got booked on a job to shoot a series of stills for a cat litter ad. A woman in a chair with her cat. The ad agency didn't like any of the chairs that the stylist provided, so I brought in a snapshot of Ernie the chair. And they loved it. The stylist hired an upholsterer to recover the chair with thick tapestry fabric he'd found in the catalog from some obscure factory in Japan—pink with gold starbursts—at a cost of four times what they would have spent on buying a chair outright, and ten times what they would have spent on renting one, but nobody batted an eye. And after the shoot, Ernie the chair came back home to our condo—my condo—where he didn't look like shit, not anymore, but he certainly didn't fit in with the rest of the furniture.

Grace says Ernie the chair is fine, but she refuses to sit in him, and for a while there she tried to get me to stop calling him Ernie the chair. But I held my ground, and eventually, she and Ernie the chair entered into a kind of detente, where neither one acknowledges the existence of the other.

Of course I notice. I can't help but notice. So to make it up to Ernie the chair, I sit in him pretty much whenever Grace isn't around. The thing is, and I hate to admit it, she isn't entirely wrong. Ernie the chair really isn't all that comfortable. Rather than sit like a normal person, I have to do this thing where I sort of lie across, my back against one arm, my feet dangling over the other. I like to think it makes me look like a sultan, at least a sultan from an old Persian painting I'd seen once somewhere. I know better than to ask Grace to corroborate the impression.

Where was I?

Morning ritual.

Grace always manages to sleep through my morning ritual, so she can't mount a convincing argument for me to make a change. Still, I'm always careful to close the bedroom door behind me after I shower and dress.

I don't know what's different about this morning, but this morning it occurs to me that all of my morning rituals, from the toilet to the ficus to taking a shower to making my morning cappuccino, all of them involve water. The annoying bird outside seems to chirp some version of "that's what I've been trying to tell you" and then stops.

THERE'S A LINE to check out, but it moves quickly, even with only one desk clerk to manage it. She's young, probably no more than twenty, with long Polynesian hair and a hibiscus tucked behind her ear. She moves efficiently and smoothly.

I step into line while Grace, Nadine, and Evan wander over to the lobby entrance. I can hear the surf from beyond them, a constant, gentle hush, rising and falling rhythmically like the sea is breathing, a little stuffed up.

When it's my turn, she takes my key, swipes it in a reader, and drops it into a cardboard box with all the other room keys she's collected so far. Her name tag says Dorothea. The printer on the counter stutters awake, then spits out page after page of room charges. She hands the sheaf over to me and, knowing that I'm supposed to, I accept it. She says a number, a five figure number, one that represents the amount I'm supposed to pay and I've already reached into my jacket for my wallet and I'm in the process of handing my credit card over—my forearm describing an arc toward her waiting hand—when one of the line items on the top sheet jumps out at me.

Movie. $24.99.

Movie?

"Um, I don't think this is ours," I say to her, to Dorothea. She takes the credit card from my fingers anyway and swipes it through the payment processing dongle thing and then takes the paper back, examines it closely.

"Alex Jamieson?" she asks.

"Yes, that's me."

"And you were in 1402."

"Yes, but look." I hold the paper out at arm's length so I can see the printing clearly, point to the line item I'd noticed. As I do, I notice several others. Movies. All $24.99.

"See this? It says movie. We didn't rent any movies."

Dorothea gets a troubled look on her face, pulls the sheet up to her face. God, remember when you could do that? Actually read a piece of paper without having to stretch your arm all the way out?

"Ah," she says. It comes out almost like a chirp. "Got it. These were rented by... room 1623. Mr. and Mrs. Desmond."

"Then why is it on my bill?"

"I'm sorry, Mr. Jamieson. Didn't you make arrangements to be responsible for their charges?"

"Oh. Right. Yes. Never mind." I take the paper back, reach into my other jacket pocket for my reading glasses. I can feel the line behind me tensing. "Oh, one of those," the feeling seems to be.

But I've started, so I have to finish. I flip through the pages, looking over the list of charges. The ones for Evan and Nadine have their room number in parentheses between the line item and the amount, and fully three quarters of the charges are theirs. Three massages (with very generous tips), room service seven times (with generous tips), in-room movies (which you can't tip on, but if there were a way, I have a feeling Evan and Nadine would have found it), several bottles of champagne, even the cab Evan and Nadine had taken from the airport to the hotel somehow made it onto the bill.

This isn't right, I think. The look on the desk clerk's face seems to convey the same thought, although the source of her discomfort might not be the charges but rather the man holding them.

I glance over to where Grace is standing at the entrance with Evan and Nadine, the three of them laughing. They look like something out of a credit card ad, all color-coordinated in breezy vacation clothes, a lifestyle shoot, enjoying now, not worried about later, when the bill would have to be paid. They're lit, perfectly, not by some fireplug of a gaffer and his greasy nephew, the way they always seem to be when I have to hire local crews, but by God, if there is a God, and if there is he's one hell of a gaffer, the way the sunlight from outside gives them a glow around the edges, just three, maybe three and a half stops more than their skin tones. A hell of a gaffer, but totally unreliable.

Makes me think of a bit of wisdom I was given by Janusz, the instructor I studied with that summer in Tuscany. "Find the light, and the image will give herself to you," Janusz said. Janusz had a way of speaking like a Zen master. He traveled light—nothing more than two ancient camera bodies—one with a 16 and the other with a 105—and enough film canisters to fill a single lead-lined bag, no flash, no meter, no tripod, no fill, and with this he'd become a fixture, a regular contributing photographer to *National Geographic*, *Time*, and *Newsweek*. An artist.

I wanted to be an artist. We all did, all of us who paid the money and took the time off to study with Janusz. All of us with our camera bags full of gear.

That summer had not turned me into an artist. But it had turned me into a photographer. A real one. I'd already been making a decent living shooting headshots for actors and weddings and the occasional lifestyle piece for one of the local papers, but like all the other students who paid $5,000 to attend, I dreamed of doing the glamorous work, of shooting exotic locations on assignment.

We slept in dorm-like rooms in a dilapidated farmhouse somewhere outside of Monticiano and piled into two beat-up vans before dawn every day. We were driven around the hill towns for two months, shooting during the day, processing our film in the evening, and comparing our work at night.

It might have been the happiest time of my life.

I remember the feeling, writing the check. At the time I had $4,721.07 in my account, I remember exactly, and I was hoping, praying, that Tony, this real estate agent I'd just met, would come through on his offer to hire me to shoot three listings for $100 apiece before the check got cashed. Remarkable how cavalier I could be now, today, dropping nearly ten times as much on a whim. The more you have, the easier it is to throw away, I realize.

Someone in the line behind me waiting to check out clears his throat.

"Will there be anything else, Mr. Jamieson?" Dorothea asks, sliding the charge card receipt for me to sign. I notice there's a line where I can add a tip.

I don't respond, not fast enough, so Dorothea tries again. "Would you like me to recycle that?" she asks, holding her hand out for the sheaf of charges.

"Recycle?" I think. That's funny. Not funny enough to make me smile. I sign, slide the charge receipt back to the desk clerk. I wonder if I should put a zero in the tip line, or at least write the total underneath, but I already feel like an asshole. She looks honest, Dorothea, I tell myself.

She dismisses me with a smile, moving her eyes to the person waiting in line behind me before I can smile back. Which is fine. I don't feel like smiling back.

I fold the pages of room charges into quarters, shove them into the pocket with the reading glasses, and walk toward the entrance.

As I approach, Grace, Evan, and Nadine turn as one, their

smiles remaining but becoming artificial. Plastic.

"What took so long?" Grace kids. This would be the time to say something, but I don't take it. I shrug, as if I don't know.

"Did you guys get a cab?" I ask.

"Naw," guffaws Evan, like the very notion is ridiculous. "We were waiting for you!"

THE YACHT IS HUGE, gleaming white. It's parked right near the front, alongside the other beautiful yachts, its name written on the bow in lettering that looks proud: *Feckless*. The smaller boats—the ones that go out for the day, the ones used for fishing and maintenance—are relegated to the outer docks.

The captain meets us at the gangplank. He tells us his name is Ansel, reaches his hand toward Evan. Makes sense. Evan dresses nicer than I do. Evan doesn't correct him, though. He shakes Ansel's hand and makes small talk, and it's only when Ansel makes a comment about the booking that Evan demurs. "Oh yeah," he says to Ansel like they're old friends, "This is Alex."

I hardly have time to go over what we're—I'm—hoping to do when Grace and Nadine come up and Grace tells Ansel what a pretty boat he has.

"Why, thank you," he replies. "But this is a yacht."

"A yacht? What makes it a yacht?" she asks. She sounds genuinely interested. She's good at that. She has this way of looking into your eyes when she talks to you, like you're the most important person in the world. Like you're the only person in the world. I love when she looks at me like that.

"A yacht is a boat that can't fit on another boat," he explains. "Here, let me show you around." He says it to all of us, but it feels like he's saying it directly to Grace.

It's moments like this that I envy, moments when Grace opens conversations with complete strangers and makes them feel close, special.

When we first decided to move in together, when she first agreed to move into my condo, we went to dinner at Shoyu, my favorite Japanese restaurant. The waitress is this tall blonde who somehow assimilated the deferential attitude and mannerisms typical of Japanese women. It's always bizarre hearing her implicitly apologizing, bowing, and receding, all the while speaking with a German accent. It's one of the things I love about this place. The food is good, but the simple act of ordering is entertaining, in the way that reading a book or watching a sunset is.

"What's your name?" Grace asked the waitress when she came over to take our order.

"Ana," she replied.

"Such a pretty name. Where are you from?"

This is a skill I'm utterly deficient in. I might have eventually found out about Ana, that she was from Hamburg and that she'd moved to LA to study art and liked it, so she decided to stay, but I wouldn't have done so at our first meeting the way Grace did. And I certainly wouldn't have ended up having a fifteen-minute conversation that culminated with inviting her to have coffee tomorrow.

Who am I kidding? I'd never eventually find out about Ana. And Ana would never find out about me. Not if it weren't for Grace.

I tip well. I'd learned—hoped, really—that doing so would get me better tables, faster service, bigger portions. There's no evidence that it does, though. And for good reason. The tip comes afterward. So if I have to wait forty-five minutes for my order, really all I'm doing is reinforcing that it doesn't matter.

What Grace does is up front. She has a way of charming people, disarming them. And with it comes exactly the kind of treatment I hope to get.

Now that I think of it, Grace did that with me, too, and when she did, I thought she found me fascinating. But I wonder if she just treats everyone that way. Like it's simply her default setting.

Still, even if she treated me the same as everyone else, it's to my home, my bed, that she returns at the end of the day. And doesn't that make me special?

Grace hadn't decided what she wanted yet, so Ana gave us a couple more minutes with the menus. But instead of looking it over, Grace asked me, "If you could be any kind of animal, what would you be?"

"A pelican," I answered without hesitating. It was something I'd thought about before.

She gave a little sneer. "A pelican? Why?"

I felt the need to defend my choice. "I love pelicans. They're noble. They don't fuck with anybody and pretty much nobody fucks with them. They fly solo, but they're good hooking up with some other pelicans if they all happen to be going the same way. And they eat sushi," I added, with a nod toward the sushi bar I like to hang out at when I grab lunch alone.

"You don't like sushi," she accused playfully.

"Sure I do."

"I've never seen you eat it."

"Because I know you don't like it."

"That's..." She couldn't come up with a word. Looking back, I wonder if the word she was looking for was "pathetic."

"Besides," I said, trying to move the conversation toward the self-deprecating, "they have big noses." Self-deprecation usually works. With other people, anyway. Not so much with her.

"Mmm hmm," she agreed.

There was an awkward silence. One that other women

might fill with "You don't have a big nose," or maybe "I love your big nose."

I tried again. "How about you? What animal would you be?"

"A dolphin."

I knew what she would say to explain why, but I asked anyway.

"Because they're beautiful," she started. Yep. I was right. "And they're smart and sassy and everybody loves them."

"I can see that," I said, even though I couldn't. Sure, dolphins are charming, at least as apex predators go, but that doesn't diminish the fact that they're ruthless killers who hunt in packs. I wanted to say, "Dolphins have big noses, too," but I didn't. Of course I didn't.

After that, we sat, silent. I had no idea what might be going through her mind, but I hoped it wasn't that she regretted agreeing to move in. I tried not to allow any expression of concern to cross my face.

When Ana came back to take our order, she brought gyoza. Grace ordered teriyaki chicken. I followed suit. I thought about ordering sushi, now that it was out in the open that I actually liked it, but it felt like I'd be doing it to prove a point, not because it's what I actually wanted.

As Ana headed back to the kitchen, smiling, it occurred to me that, like pelicans, dolphins eat pretty much nothing but raw fish. I didn't point it out. I couldn't. We'd moved on from that topic of conversation. And even if we hadn't, I wasn't sure I could bring it up without coming across as petty.

A LOT OF PEOPLE have a romantic notion of what it would be like to sail a yacht across the ocean, and I was one of them. Until I actually got here.

It's boring.

Every direction you look, it's water all the way to the horizon. You're making progress—you know you are because you can see the way the bow splits the water and little waves splash off to the sides, the rhythmic shhhhhh, shhhhhh, shhhhhh, like the ocean is asking, urging, demanding that you keep a secret. But yachts, even fast yachts, don't go all that fast. It feels like you're pretty much standing still in a breeze and not even a particularly stiff one, even when you're at top speed.

And while a sixty-foot yacht sounds big when you're looking at how much it costs to rent it, you're only about thirty-five minutes into the voyage before the novelty has worn off. There's just not a whole lot new to see or do. You've already rifled through all the board games and puzzles in the galley and you've perused all the books and old magazines. You've looked over the ropes and knots and figured out what they're attached to. There's no cell service or internet connection, so you can't text with friends or update your Facebook page, and even if you could, what would you say? "Still bored." With an emoji that expressed ennui, if they made one.

So you develop your own rituals.

Evan takes to using his fingernail to pick at peeling paint wherever he finds it. Nadine does yoga, sometimes holding a downward dog pose for what seems like hours, but is probably closer to minutes. Grace comes out on deck, looks around, and sighs. Then she disappears down below. And me? I sit on the deck, leaning my back against what I'd learned is called a bulkhead, my eyes closed, listening to the rhythm of the water. I can shut out the light, but despite the way the water constantly urges them to hush, I can't help but hear the other ritual of my traveling companions, their complaining. They must figure I'm asleep because they don't bother to keep their voices down, not even when they're almost on top of me.

Whatever.

The consensus seems to be that this is a stupid idea and a waste of money, and if I really wanted to waste money, I could option any number of screenplays that Evan represents or hire a crew to shoot the one-woman show that Nadine is convinced will revitalize her career but hasn't got around to writing, or at the very least, fill a Michael Kors bag with cash and hand it to Grace so she can go buy something she deserves.

I'm careful to slather my skin with sunscreen, but even so, the air is so clear that the rays feel like they pierce through. Good sunscreen, though. My skin doesn't even turn pink.

Shhhhhh, shhhhhh, shhhhhh...

Maybe I doze off because I'm surprised by a Bap-Bap! I open my eyes to see that the sun is touching the horizon, and it's Ansel rapping on the door to the bridge announcing dinner. As I get up, the others cast furtive glances my way. I pretend not to notice, pretend not to have been awake the whole time, and do my best to cast a friendly smile in the direction of anybody who might be looking my way. Generally it's only Ansel, but by the third day, even that stops.

Nights are worse.

Or maybe better.

There's nothing to see, unless you like looking up at a sky so filled with stars it seems to glow gray, which is actually cool, but after a while, even that loses its luster.

Shhhhhh, shhhhhh, shhhhhh...

And then it begins.

It begins as giggling, quiet and occasional, interrupted by a whispered playful admonishment to hush. A sixty-foot yacht is pretty small. Smaller than the entire apartment I lived in when I got that first job in New York, that studio walk-up on what I called the Upper East Side because I didn't want Mom to worry about me, but which was really past the border, on the other side of the invisible line that separated the safe from the unsafe, the consumers from the producers. I used to joke that my apartment was so small that I could lie in bed and do the dishes, but it really wasn't a joke. And that apartment was bigger than this entire boat.

Yacht.

After dinner, Ansel pours me a tumbler of bourbon—a nice gesture, an acknowledgment, maybe, that yes, I appreciate that you hired me. He doesn't pour a drink for anyone else. Not that he denies them any. Evan, Nadine, and Grace know they're welcome to anything in the galley, and Evan and Nadine take full advantage of the tequila and rum, but the bourbon Ansel pours for me doesn't come from the galley. The galley has a bottle of Maker's Mark, which is fine, but the first evening, when I poured myself a couple of fingers, Ansel must have noticed me making a face because he went into his own cabin and came out with a glass and handed it silently to me.

I don't really know much about bourbon. I know enough to know that I like Knob Creek and Woodford Reserve, but I'm no connoisseur. But this bourbon, whatever it is, the bourbon that Ansel keeps in his private stash, is exceptional.

After dinner, everybody goes off in their own directions.

Ansel sets about cleaning the galley and I end up on the deck, my back to the bulkhead, sipping my bourbon.

The giggling soon gives way to moaning. Even that's fairly quiet, so quiet that you have to strain your ears to hear it over the rush of water by the hull. But the moaning, female moaning, gets louder, more urgent. It isn't long before all modesty is abandoned and the moaning goes full-on porno, rhythmic, interrupted with all the cliches: "Give it to me!" "Harder, faster!" "Oh yes! Oh God!"

Maybe Nadine is rehearsing her one-woman show after all.

Then climax, and then silence. Except for the water. Shhhhhh, shhhhhh, shhhhhh...

Hearing other people having sex is embarrassing, more for me than for Nadine and Evan, although I'm not sure why that should be. When the giggling turns to moaning, I close my eyes, pretend to sleep. If anyone were to come out onto the deck, I wouldn't want them to catch me listening.

Not that anyone ever comes out onto the deck. Not until afterward. Ten, maybe fifteen minutes afterward, I hear the hatch open and I close my eyelids again, enough that I look like I'm asleep, but open just enough to be able to see. It's Ansel. Always and only Ansel. He looks out onto the deck, holding his own glass of bourbon. He gives me this look, like he's sizing me up, and when he's satisfied that I'm asleep, he turns and goes back belowdeck.

This. This is how I choose to blow several dozen thousand dollars.

It's kind of depressing when you think about it. And when I can't stand thinking about it anymore, sitting under the judgmental glare of the stars anymore, I hoist myself up, drain the last of the bourbon, and go belowdeck. I leave the glass on the table in the galley and make my way to the cabin.

By the time I get in, Grace is already asleep, her mouth open, face smushed against the pillow. She's kind of not all that attractive when she sleeps, but I'm grateful that she's sleeping. Otherwise, she'd tell me that her back is killing her or that she has a raging headache. I undress down to my boxers and climb into the bed.

Last night, the third night out, Grace moved when she felt me get into the bed. Last night, she actually reached out and put her hand on my chest. She didn't wake and I didn't want to do anything to disturb the moment. But it made me smile. Yeah, it cost lots of thousands of dollars, I think, but what a small price to pay.

Tonight, though. Tonight, as I sit on the deck, pretending to be asleep, eavesdropping on Evan and Nadine having sex somewhere below, the hatch opens in the middle of the performance. At the point just as she's about to climax. I keep my eyelids closed but open enough to see. It isn't Ansel. Wouldn't be anyway. For some reason, Ansel never appears until after the orgasm.

And then I see why. It's Evan and Nadine. They poke their heads out just in time to hear an ecstatic "Oh God!" louder and clearer because the voice carries through the open hatch, out into the still, clear night.

"Oh God!" Evan and Nadine exclaim in hushed response, in unison. If this were a movie, if this were written into one of the scripts Evan pimps around Hollywood, it would definitely be a comedy, but this isn't a movie. Evan and Nadine share an embarrassed look and duck back belowdecks, closing the hatch as quietly as they can. At least now I'm not the only one embarrassed.

I don't move. How could I? Where would I go? Tears force their way through my eyelids, eyelids that I had closed, but not enough to keep out the truth.

Suddenly, I want to be off the boat, even if it means throwing myself into the water. And I would, except that Ansel told us that tomorrow at dawn we'd be arriving. Arriving at my destination. The island of garbage.

How fitting.

WHEN DAWN COMES, I find myself at the bow of the *Feckless* as the yacht bobs just off the shore of what could be a lovely tropical island—and not a small one at that. It looks like Bora Bora, like pictures you see of Bora Bora anyway, maybe ten miles across, rising in a lumpy ridge topped by a peak that rises even higher from its middle. It's beautiful.

I gasp at the sight. And that's when I say, "I'm going to make this mine."

I have no idea Grace is behind me. I hadn't seen her, spoken to her, since dinner the night before. I stayed out on the deck, and everyone else, even or maybe especially Ansel, had given me a wide berth.

"Of course you are," she says.

It's beautiful, this island, until you look closely, which Grace had obviously done. When you look closely, you can see that those aren't black sand beaches; they're thousands and thousands of trash bags. That isn't lush tropical foliage; it's piles of discarded appliances. The entire landmass isn't a landmass at all.

It's garbage.

I know I should be angry, but I don't feel angry. I don't feel relieved, either. Weary, maybe. I ignore her and carry my bags to the gangway that leads to the not-beach. When I return to collect the next load, she's gone.

I take the provisions I'd packed, one by one, from the hold to the gangway and down, placing them on the floe. A plastic floe. I think about that story they tell about Eskimos, what they do with old people. How when you get to be too old to contribute—when you consume more than you produce—you're placed on an ice floe and left to float away, no longer a burden on the community's resources. No credit bestowed for the years you gave more than you took.

Nobody offers me a hand as I take all the provisions I'd packed in the hold and carry them down the ladder. When I get everything down, I do one more sweep of the *Feckless* to see if there's anything I missed. I find Evan, Nadine, and Grace in the galley, drinks and the satellite phone on the table in front of them, an open Pottery Barn catalog on the table, Grace in the middle of a gesture as if she'd stopped talking mid-story.

The three of them say nothing as I come in. Evan and Nadine can't bring their eyes to meet mine. Grace leaves her hand in the air like she's waiting to pick up the story exactly where she'd been cut off as soon as I'm finished interrupting her. The catalog is open to a page showing overstuffed chairs, and the one that's featured looks like a knock-off of Ernie the chair.

I pick up the satellite phone, return it to its case.

"You're taking the satellite phone?" Grace asks. Her voice is incredulous.

"Um, yeah."

"Seriously?"

"Yeah, seriously."

She expels a huff. "You're doing this to punish me."

"No, I'm doing this in case I need it. I'm camping on a raft of garbage in the middle of the ocean, thousands of miles from anything."

"Well, I think it's selfish."

"Of course you do," I think to myself. I'm careful not to say the words out loud. I put the case under my arm and turn to leave.

"If you get into trouble, don't expect me to help."

I wouldn't. As I get to the ladder, I wonder if those will turn out to be the last words we speak to each other. If they are, and I'm pretty sure they will be, they'd be fitting. "If you get into trouble, don't expect me to help." Yeah, that pretty much sums up the relationship.

Back on the floe, I take in my provisions. It feels woefully inadequate, and yeah, it probably is, but if the choice is to stay on the yacht, in that world...

Ansel appears at the top of the ladder, carrying a duffel bag. I glare, but he doesn't glare back. He isn't actually thinking of joining me on the garbage, is he?

He climbs down the ladder, places the duffel bag next to the rest, then returns to the *Feckless*, not saying a word.

"That's not mine," I say to myself once Ansel is gone.

"It is now," I respond to myself.

"What do you suppose is in it?"

"Your laundry?"

"No, I packed my laundry in..."

"I know that. I was joking."

The engine starts up, revs like a motorcycle, like Dan's motorcycle when he's off to cruise for fat chicks. If there's a time to change my mind, this would be it. Well, actually, no. If there was a time to change my mind, it was well past. Even if I shouted, I know nobody on board would admit to hearing me over the sound of the engine. The *Feckless* pulls away.

"If you get into trouble, don't expect me to help."

I watch the *Feckless* turn its back on me, power off toward the horizon. Now that I'm not on board, it seems to move faster. A lot faster. In less than a minute, it's nothing more than a white speck on a field of blue. Blue above, blue below.

I open the duffel bag and find a coil of rope, a reel of fishing line, several fishing hooks—their points stuck into a scrap of cardboard—a metal canister of matches, a hunting knife—like the one Rambo has between his teeth in that poster—in a worn canvas sheath, and two heavy-duty plastic cases. In the very corner, a faded T-shirt, wadded-up, like maybe it's laundry after all, only it isn't one of mine. There's no note.

The plastic cases hold a flare gun and a dozen flares. I've seen flare guns in movies, but I've never touched one. I'm tempted to stick a flare into the gun and fire it.

"You should shoot one," my self tells me.

"Why?" I answer.

"So you know how it works, in case you end up needing it."

"What if they see it and come back?"

"Right." They wouldn't come back, even if they saw it.

"If I shoot one, I'll be down a flare if I end up needing it."

"Which won't make a difference if you don't know how to make it go."

In the end, I decide to read the manual. I follow the instructions, placing a flare into the chamber but not actually pulling the trigger.

"Pull the trigger."

"No."

"What if it doesn't work?"

"What if it doesn't? I'm going to what? Take it in and have it fixed?"

"Well, at least you'll know."

At least you'll know. The words seem to bounce around, to echo inside my empty skull.

At least you'll know.

"Maybe I don't want to know," I reply quietly to myself.

I place the flare gun and the flares back into their cases and the cases back in the duffel bag. Then I reach for the wadded up T-shirt. It isn't wadded. It's wrapped around something.

An unopened bottle of Burnside Bourbon.

So that's what the bourbon was. A little distillery out of Portland, Oregon, making six different styles of bourbon, each in its own colorful bottle. I'd been hired to shoot a collateral package for the brand, but I didn't get a chance to taste it because as soon as I called wrap, the prop master spirited away the six bottles the client had provided for the shoot and I didn't get a chance to taste a sip.

You can get the stuff in LA, but it's pricey, double what I pay for the bourbons I know I like just fine and besides, with six different varieties, I couldn't begin to know which one to try. So I never take a chance and buy a bottle.

But there it is, finally, and yeah, when you add in the yacht and the hotel in Hawaii and the airfare and the movies that Evan and Nadine rented, it's pretty damn expensive.

WHEN TONY CALLED to tell me he'd decided to sell the studio, I didn't respond. I didn't know what to say. The silence must have been uncomfortable for him. "I told you from the beginning this was a property play," Tony reminded me. And he had. The city had funded an arts grant that would subsidize the down payment on the purchase of unused industrial space. You just needed to occupy the space and "make art," whatever that meant, for ten years, after which the loan would be forgiven.

I didn't really know Tony very well when he proposed going into business together. I'd been his go-to photographer to shoot listings, and as Tony's listings got bigger, I never bothered to raise my rates. A hundred bucks to shoot a house was fine, and to be honest, the nicer houses are a lot easier to shoot. You don't have to worry about personal shit that has to be hidden or walls that need to be repainted. Sure, it's more rooms, but they're clean, well furnished, and generally pretty well lit.

After a couple of years, Tony got into commercial real estate and those shoots were even easier. Mostly big empty spaces, where the main assignment was to give a sense of scale. We'd meet maybe once a month at Hugo's Coffee, a block away from Tony's office, just long enough to drink a cup. I liked those meetings, that they felt almost clandestine, like we were doing some kind of illicit transaction, making superficial conversation about the weather or Tony's kids while sliding envelopes across the small table to each other: Tony's envelope with a check and mine with photos.

Then one day Tony asked to grab a cup when there hadn't been anything to shoot for a while. It was weird not making small talk, not passing envelopes to each other. Instead, he asked me about my art. And that threw me.

First off, I always had a hard time thinking of photography as art. I mean, I always wanted to be an artist, but in my mind, art is something you make, and photography is weird. You aren't actually making anything. You're seeing what's out there and choosing the framing and the moment to capture it, sure, but what are you actually making?

So while yes, I'm always shooting my own stuff, looking for interesting images, I'm never sure if it really qualifies as art.

Tony told me that didn't matter. "Art is whatever you decide it is," he said. I never quite thought of it that way.

I offered to show Tony the stuff I was working on, but he said whatever. He just told me about the idea of building a studio and asked if I'd be interested.

Would I? Of course I would. It was like Tony was actually giving me permission to be an artist. We shook hands and it was a deal. No contract or anything.

What I didn't realize—only now do I realize, now that the studio is gone—was that what Tony was actually giving me was an opportunity to be the opposite, a not-artist. And what Tony didn't realize, couldn't realize, was that I happened to be the perfect not-artist to build a studio with.

Tony gave me permission to be an artist, but it was Janusz, the artist, who gave me what I needed to be a not-artist.

It was our second day in Italy, when the vans drove us into Sienna. The vans parked outside the city walls, and Janusz led us toward the center, where the Palio di Siena was coming up. Most of the other students were excited at the prospect. They'd heard that several of the teams would be practicing and they hoped to get shots of the horses galloping on the cobblestones of the ancient city or, at the very least, of the preparations being made. But Janusz pulled us up short as we crossed one of the city's cavernous streets. He made everyone look over to the left, where the 700-year-old buildings on one side glowed.

When everybody fell silent, Janusz pointed. "Light, she only travel in a straight line," he said. Which yeah, everybody knows. But then he added, "You are illuminated. And so you reflect."

Pow! It was a fucking revelation.

The other students snapped photos from where they stood, like paparazzi at the Academy Awards, but Janusz didn't. I didn't either. I stared, fucking dumbstruck, trying to figure out how the light got from the sun onto the buildings.

Light travels in a straight line, but it bounces off of everything it hits, and here, the way the street curved, the way the clouds had settled in, it was like having a huge Fisher box, like the ones you use to light cars, but on its side, which of course you'd never do with a car because then you wouldn't get the definition in the fenders.

The rest of the students moved on, but I stayed. Light, she only travel in a straight line. Whatever it hits is both illuminated and reflects. There. There was the secret.

Reflecting and illuminating. Illuminating and reflecting.

From that moment on, I found myself paying special attention to the lessons Janusz imparted, especially the ones he sort of tossed out there, like casual observations. There were so many of them and I wish I'd written them all down. I'd forget one for years, and then find myself in a difficult situation and it would come bubbling back up.

It didn't happen right away, but after that day in Sienna studio lighting became intuitive. You could light something and at the same time use it to reflect, to light something else. It became so simple. Breakfast cereal, fish bowls, bathrooms, cars—objects and spaces that would cause other photographers to tear their hair out, adding flags and scrims and fill and dinks until you'd have to pick your way through a warren of stands and cables to get to the thing being shot—I figured out how to do it simpler, faster, and cheaper. And Tony offered me the opportunity to do it.

It wasn't glamorous by any means. I never got to shoot half-naked models because anybody can light skin. And I never got to go on location to Paris or Prague or London because the light there is so beautiful, so diffuse, and the backgrounds so evocative that you never need to do much more than get the exposure right (f16 at the ISO, minus one stop, if you manage not to have a light meter on you, and you're good to go).

In ten years Tony never came by the studio. He hooked me up with Kathryn, took care of all the financial stuff from his fancy office so that I was free to be the artist; that's how he always put it. And that's how it was. And if I wasn't being an artist, it was my own damn fault. The checks came quarterly and some quarters I made more than a lot of people made in a year. Hell, in three years.

But then Tony sold the building and hired some guy out of Houston to auction off all the equipment and I got a big fat check. A big fat check for $3.7 million, which took me completely by surprise. I called Tony right away, asking him nervously to meet at Hugo's.

I brought the check with me, in case it was a mistake and Tony wanted it back.

My surprise took Tony by surprise, and maybe I was a little too grateful at the amount because at first Tony acted defensive, like maybe I was being sarcastic, like maybe I thought I was getting screwed. Tony defended the amount, telling me that was what our deal had been going in and I could look through the books if I wanted to, to see that the number had been arrived at correctly. Not that I would. I'd never asked to so much as look over a budget for a job I'd been hired to shoot, and even if I had, I wouldn't know what to look for and I said as much to Tony. After an uncomfortable couple of minutes, Tony eased up.

"Enjoy the money," Tony said. "Figure out what you want to do next. Go be an artist." He let me pay for the coffee and left without finishing his.

With a few million in the bank, I didn't need to worry. At first. But it had been six months now, and even though I'd booked a couple of gigs—mostly with art directors I shot for before—it didn't exactly give me the kind of income I could live on.

Still, it takes a while to spend down $3.7 million. It would be a while before I ran out.

IT'S QUIET NOW that the *Feckless* is gone. Eerily quiet. I realize I'd become so accustomed to the thrum of the yacht's engine that its absence is a presence. The only sound is the repetitive hush of the water lapping at the shore.

Shhhhhh, shhhhhh, shhhhhh...

Every direction looks the same. Blue above, blue below. Every direction except behind. Behind it's blue above, whitish below. An undulating whitish expanse. The sun glints off of irregular pieces of plastic that coalesced into a glittering landmass.

A thought pops into my mind. "How very much like my career," I hear myself say. "Putting sparkle onto garbage."

So here I am, at my destination. And now what? When you reach your goal, what do you do next? Celebrate? Set a new goal?

"Go be an artist," Tony commanded. Despite all of the anticipation, I realize I'm totally not prepared.

I scan the horizon at the point where the *Feckless* had disappeared. Nothing. It's long gone.

And then it occurs to me. You know what? I should be on the boat. I should have stayed on the boat and I should have made the others get off, every last one of them. I'm the one who chartered the boat. I'm the one who Grace cheated on. I'm the victim. And here I am, making the decision to embrace my victimhood. Not just embrace it, but take it to the next level. It isn't enough to be taken advantage of; I had to allow—enable—that advantage to be multiplied.

Whatever.

How is this different from any other time in my life?

You know what sucks? Nobody tried to stop me. Nobody expressed concern. Nobody offered to help. The only objection came from Grace when she found out I was taking the satellite phone.

And why would they? I packed the case of water, the box of PowerBars, the desalination thing, the tarps, the life preserver, the heavy-weather gear. For all the conversations I'd had with myself, I never admitted it: this was the plan all along.

Now would be a pretty good time to feel despair, I think. I'm probably going to die here. Nobody will even know. Well, not exactly nobody. But the people who will know, Evan and Nadine and Grace, they'll be too wrapped up in themselves to even bother thinking about it. And certainly won't feel any guilt over it. The only one who showed any kind of concern was Ansel. The duffel bag—what was that for? To assuage his guilt? To take responsibility? To ensure that the check would clear?

The thing is, I don't really feel despair. Anger maybe. But even that, not anger powerful enough to make me do anything, not that there's anything I can do. Besides, I like the silence, the solitude.

I stare out at the water. The infinite water.

Something about this makes me think of the night Janusz called off the critique. We'd been to Florence—of course we'd been to Florence. You can't go to Tuscany and not see Florence. More than half of the people in our little workshop had taken the same photo of a red Vespa parked in front of a stone wall.

Seven of us managed to get a shot of a couple sitting at a café table, looking out onto a piazza. And five people, myself included, took a shot of a pair of old men playing backgammon outside a doorway. So very Italian. The men were happy to pose, happy to take 5 euros from me for their trouble. Maggie gave them 10 euros, and Warren—I think his name was Warren—gave them twenty. All in all, they made 58 euros that day from us alone, which we all laughed about. None of the shots did exactly what we wanted them to—the Vespa wasn't parked quite right, the couple was sitting at a plastic table festooned with logos for Marlboro cigarettes, and the old men, charming as they were, looked more like retired American middle managers than Italian grandpas. And that's when Janusz called the critique off. He was angry, you could tell.

"Real photographer is no looking for picture in your head, picture somebody else already take," he yelled before storming out. "See what is! Not what you hope!"

"You know..." I hear myself say to myself.

"Shut up."

I don't want to think about "See what is! Not what you hope!" so I do a quick inventory of my stuff. Everything is there. Like it matters. If something is missing, what am I going to do about it? Still, it's a habit I developed over years of traveling solo. I learned through experience that nobody else is going to take any responsibility for me or my things.

And why should they? For the studio work, the assignments I shot in other places, I'd write up an order and there'd be camera equipment waiting for me there. Usually medium- or large-format Mamiya. My own gear, the Canon with the 16-30, the 85, and the 70-210, those are the tools I use to shoot my own personal stuff. The "art" that Tony used to score the grant.

I never even saw the application that Tony submitted for that grant. I sweated about it for weeks, putting together a portfolio of work that Tony could show to the city, to help justify the decision to provide the funding. When I brought it by his fancy office, two weeks before the deadline to submit the application, Tony took it without even opening the case to see the work inside. Like he wasn't sure what he was supposed to do with it.

Almost nine months later, after the grant had been secured and the former canning plant had been bought and built out, I came into the office Tony had built for me behind the cyc wall and found the portfolio on the desk. I wondered if it had ever been opened.

Tony even hired a studio manager to run the jobs that came in, a woman named Fran who hadn't ever run a studio but did manage a meat packing facility in Ohio. Fran was always looking for a way to maximize profits, and if that meant bidding a job to be shot in Argentina because the models there didn't have to be paid union wages, she was on it. I didn't mind. I got to travel a lot. Not necessarily to the kinds of exotic places I would have liked to visit, but I shot in Detroit and Halifax and Atlanta more times than I can count because Fran knew how to work the tax breaks that the governments there gave for production. When I booked jobs with ad agencies in New York, I ended up shooting a lot in New Jersey—Hoboken and Jersey City—because the studios there were close enough for the clients to visit, but were a lot cheaper than the ones in Soho and Tribeca.

Fran always booked my travel, too, and I always ended up in coach, usually in a middle seat at the back of the plane. But it was fine. Sure, some photographers command production assistants who meet them at the airport and whisk them to their four-star hotels in a limo, but I was always left on my own, to hail a cab and carry my own bag.

This time, though, it's something else, something more. I need to reassure myself that my camera bag is there. And there it is, the shoulder strap lashed securely to a float that probably isn't buoyant enough to keep it from sinking.

Something Janusz told our group when we met up the week before we boarded the plane for Italy. A kid—some spoiled rich kid who wanted to shoot models so he could get laid—Warren? Was his name Warren? Why can't I remember that kid's name? Whatever. Doesn't matter. Warren was frustrated that his work wasn't coming together and figured a new camera would be the solution. He couldn't decide between the new top-of-the-line Nikon and the new top-of-the-line Canon, and he asked Janusz for advice. Janusz said, "Best camera is the one you are holding in your hand," saying it in a sage voice, a voice that sounded sad, actually. But sometimes, criticism is too subtle for the person being criticized to understand. The kid showed up at the airport with both cameras, with a complete set of top-of-the-line lenses for both, and wanted Janusz to set them up for him.

It wasn't too subtle for Maggie, the determined kid who took one shot a day, but spent hours in the darkroom, dodging and burning and finessing to turn what, I'm sorry, were utterly unremarkable photos into utterly unremarkable photos with perfect tonal range. Maggie worked as an architectural photographer, and her professional work was precise and utterly uninspiring, but like me and all the others, she wanted to be an artist. As we were boarding the plane at JFK, she happened to be walking in front of me, and once we were out of range of Janusz, who had taken up the rear, she turned and said, "He didn't come up with that."

"Come up with what?" I asked, knowing full well what she was talking about.

"The thing about the best camera. It was Cartier-Bresson."

Of course she would know.

Not that it mattered.

One thing I did know was that Cartier-Bresson had also said, "Your first 10,000 photographs are your worst," but I didn't mention that to Maggie. At the rate she shot, she still had seventy-four years to go before she'd get to her first decent photograph.

But I have more than 10,000 shots under my belt. Probably more than 100,000. And yeah, the first 10,000 were shit, but so are at least 99 percent of the ones I'm currently shooting.

At least I'd switched to digital. When I did the photo workshop, the one with Janusz, my camera bag weighed twenty-four pounds, what with all the film canisters and the lead-lined pouches I kept them in—one for exposed and the other for unexposed—so that airport X-ray machines wouldn't fog the negatives.

But when I finally went to a presentation by a Canon rep—someone who used charts and graphs to show that using the same lenses, digital cameras could capture a dynamic range and detail as good as or better than film—it was obvious that going digital would allow me to get away from so much of that.

Bonus, ten SD cards hold more images than an entire two-drawer filing cabinet full of negatives.

Of course, the more you're able to shoot, the more you end up shooting. You don't have to rewind the film into the canister after twenty-four shots, so you don't have to be as careful with each one. You can keep on firing, hundreds of images, trying subtle variations of exposure or composition.

And so we do. Photographers make so many images that these days everything moves at the speed of fashion. Products, flavors, packaging—nothing that was around last year is relevant this year. You have all these images, perfect images that will last forever, but those images have absolutely no value because whatever they're images of, those things have all become obsolete.

And sure, ten SD cards can fit into a matchbox, but you can't just leave the images on the cards. You need to store them. All of them. So now my camera bag has a two-terabyte drive, sealed in a Ziploc bag, where the lead-lined bag used to be. And another two-terabyte drive in one of the pockets because you never know when one drive is going to fail. Plus a card reader and cables.

To run all this stuff requires electricity, so of course the bag is stocked with back-up batteries. Rechargeable batteries need chargers, and chargers need adapters for different countries' voltages and plug configurations. There's a solar charger, too, plus four packs of regular store-bought Duracells in their plastic-and-cardboard packages, also stuffed into Ziploc bags, in case the solar charger fails or the rechargeable batteries die.

With all this equipment, my camera bag is down to a lithe twenty-three pounds.

Progress.

And it is, really. Silver halide film is sensitive to not just light and X-rays, but heat. And once the negatives are processed, they immediately start to decay. You won't notice for ten years with Kodachrome, but Ektachrome and Velvia fall off faster, even if you store your negatives in special sleeves, in a climate-controlled environment.

There's also less room for fuck-ups. Before I switched to digital, that time I was in Guadalajara, shooting an assignment for Taco Bell—a studio shot of tortillas among sheaves of wheat—I was walking from the hotel to the studio early in the morning, and there it was. An amazing shot. A guy on a unicycle, framed by the doors to a cathedral, lit from the side by the rising sun.

I knew I had gold the instant I tripped the shutter and I spent the entire rest of the way to the studio trying to decide how to process the film. I decided that I'd cross process—develop the Velvia in chemistry designed for negative film—to give the colors a surreal feeling, but when I wound the roll onto the spool, the emulsion of that frame was squished against the plastic backing of another frame and the shot was ruined.

It was heartbreaking.

That can't happen with digital. Once you have the images, they're perfect. You can't fuck them up by winding them onto the spool wrong, agitating too vigorously or not vigorously enough, losing track of the time and not keeping the negative in there long enough or too long, or just dropping the tank and having it explode open, exposing the negative to light and splashing stinky, staining chemicals onto your pants.

Digital images are like plastic compared to the wood of analog images. They last forever. With an old-fashioned negative, no copy is as perfect as the original, but with digital, you can make infinite identical copies and spread them all over the world.

They're perfect, but they're not as good.

There's an upside to a fucked-up image. It gives you a way to brag without bragging. You don't have to wait for someone to like your shot enough to remark on it so you can talk about where you've been on assignment. Instead, you can come across as a guy who made a mistake, a mistake that just happened to be in some cool, exotic place. What's more perfect than imperfection, right?

Come to think of it, that was one of the stories I told at that party where I met a young actress fresh off the bus from Nebraska. She looked deep into my eyes, taking in my every word as I did my best to be charming. I found her beautiful—even more beautiful when she told me her name: Grace. I offered to shoot some headshots for her and that's how we started dating.

Anyway.

AS I LOOK OUT across the bleak landscape, I find myself dealing with two conflicting urges. The first is to take out the camera and shoot. I know from both Janusz and experience that the first impression of a place, any place, diminishes with familiarity. And that it's the first impression that is often the most telling. I want to capture the bleakness, the intense contrast of white against blue, before I become inured to them.

But I also need to take a crap.

I decide to compromise. I take the camera out of the bag, flick the power switch on and check the battery level (100%) and the number of shots left on the card (432), then flick it off. Then I throw the strap over my shoulder and try to figure out which direction to head.

Not that I think I'll actually find a restroom, but I hope I'll come across a spot that says "restroom" to me. A spot that I can commit to pooping in. A spot distinct from all the other spots in the indistinguishable mass of detritus.

Nothing speaks to me, so I choose a direction at random and pick my way there.

Underfoot, it's pretty solid. I mean, it squishes a bit

wherever I step, but never feels like it's going to give way. Still, I proceed carefully. Too carefully, probably, given the urgency of my bowels.

I get to a point where it feels like I either need to commit or accept that I'm going to have an accident in my shorts. The terrain is pretty flat, but a rusty forty-gallon drum protrudes from the mass—a whale breaching from among ice floes, frozen at the peak of its arc. I look back to check on my gear. It's closer than it feels like it ought to be. Surely, I must have gone farther than just this. Seems like I should have gone farther than this.

"Further," my other self corrects me.

"Further?"

"Yeah. There's a difference."

Whatever.

I chose this path and this is as far as it got me. Nothing to do now but do the thing I came here to do.

But how?

It's not like I'm uncomfortable going to the bathroom where there's no bathroom. I've shot in enough studios that had less-than-first-world amenities, and stayed in enough places where there were no facilities at all, that I'm not at all squeamish about dropping trou. But this experience isn't like any of the others.

I move the camera strap over my head so that it's slung diagonally across my chest and back, strap over one shoulder, camera below the other. Then I kneel on the plastic and begin pulling up piece after piece of garbage. Digging a hole.

You're supposed to dig a hole in the dirt, at least 100 feet from any water source, I think that's what they say in the Boy Scouts. I'm not a Boy Scout, but I read an article about the Boy Scouts on a plane once. But there's no dirt here. And this island is floating. So I'm definitely not 100 feet from the water.

On the other hand, I'm literally standing on garbage. And there's no alternative.

A faded flip flop. A plastic grocery bag. Trash bags. Milk jugs. Take-out containers. As each comes out, more seem to replace them. How deep should I dig? The Boy Scouts, I seem to remember, say to dig a hole six inches deep. Six inches down I still haven't hit water. Do I want to hit water? Would it be better to shit in the water than into the plastic? When you think about it, shitting into garbage is essentially the same as shitting into the water, but on time delay. I keep digging.

About a foot and a half down, I remove a torn fragment of a sun-bleached tarp, and there it is. Water. Blue. A deep blue. A blue that looks remarkably unsullied. Unpolluted. I suddenly regret having dug that deep, but by then it's too late. I seriously have to take a crap, and besides, how stupid would it be to replace the garbage I've removed?

I drop my shorts and turn my body so I'm facing directly away from the open water where my gear waits. Because what? Somebody might see? I squat over the hole and then immediately regret it. I forgot to pack toilet paper. Which is fine. I could use the water. Except that I'm taking a shit in the water and you don't want to clean your ass with shit water.

Meaning I'll have to wipe with shit plastic.

Ugh.

The first time I used a squat toilet was in Morocco. It was on a job for a line of disposable razors and no, I'm not making that up. Bathrooms, ironically enough, where men were meant to be portrayed enjoying shaving with these remarkable, disposable, one-time-use razors. The production team needed to build seven different bathrooms and, perversely, flying all the way to Morocco to do it was cheaper than doing it anywhere in the States.

You can't shoot in real bathrooms because real bathrooms are too small. There's no place to put the camera. So Fran found a studio in Marrakech where they could build seven of the most spectacular upper-middle-class bathrooms and, this was the part that was delicious: the studio had no bathroom.

What the studio had was a hole, a hole in a stall out in the back where goats roamed free. There was no toilet paper there, either, so I got into the practice of squirreling away napkins in my left pants pocket so I'd have something to wipe with.

But not this time.

I was surprised to find that squatting over a hole to take a crap is actually not uncomfortable at all. In fact, it actually feels more efficient. Like you're getting all the poop out of your system by having your butt so far down below your knees.

The whole time in Marrakech I got, as Tony liked to call it, a clean pinch. My poops are generally not clean pinches and I always, always need lots of toilet paper to wipe the inside of my butt cheeks. But not in Marrakech.

At the time I figured it was the food, but then when I shot that industrial container job at the port in Croatia, the same thing happened, and there I was heading back to base camp twice a day, eating at the dining tent that had been set up by production for the ad agency, which meant china and silver and the kinds of foods and snacks that the delicate flowers from New York would find not just palatable, but desirable. They say Napoleon said that an army moves on its stomach. New York ad agencies think of themselves as armies.

Still, here I am, squatting over a hole in the crust of plastic, fouling the impossibly clean water beneath it, and not sure how to finish off. So I do what I always do. I distract myself.

I sling the camera up in front of me, remove the lens cap, click on the power, and hold the viewfinder to my eye, scanning left and right to line up a composition that includes the forty-gallon drum in a pleasing manner. Then I pivot, twisting my upper torso without moving my feet, and aim into the light. Backlight. Less saturation, but more contrast. That's what people like these days. I frame a couple different ways, sometimes high in the frame to show more garbage, sometimes low to show more sky.

But I don't fire off a shot.

I replace the lens cap, click off the power, let the camera slide back to its nest under my arm, and sigh. As usual, the problem hasn't solved itself.

A pattern, I realize. I do that. When faced with something troubling, my go-to is to delay, to put off dealing with it.

I'm still squatting over the hole, finished, and I know that no delay is going to change my circumstances. No outside force is going to show up and solve my problem for me. I'm squatting on a pile of garbage with my shorts around my ankles, no napkins in my pocket, and shit clinging to the inside of my butt, and unless I do something, nothing is going to change that.

Something else Janusz told the class pops into my head, one night while we were going over that day's shooting. "Composition is about pattern," he said. "And pattern you don't interrupt is shit." He was comparing two photographs that students had taken, both of the same field of grape vines. In one, was it Warren's? Yeah. Warren. That was his name, right? In Warren's, it was just the vines, rows stretching from one side of the frame to the other. And yeah, it was pleasing the way they curved and repeated. But in the other, the student had captured a farmer, just his hat, really, as he walked between rows of grapes, there off to the right side of the frame. Not as pretty, but the second picture was indisputably more interesting.

"Wonder what made me think of that," I ask myself.

"Shit. It was weird to hear Janusz use the word shit," I answer.

I stand up. My shorts and underwear are still around my ankles. I pull one foot out, then the other.

Then I grab up my underwear and use it to clean my butt, being careful to fold the part that I already used into the interior of the wad I make. When I'm satisfied I got it all, I look down. The shorts are like two circles, like a cell that has just about finished going through mitosis at the edge of the hole.

They're new. I bought them just for this adventure. Grace's

idea. In fact, today was the first day I'd even worn them, snapping the plastic thread that held the price tag to the waistband and then, looking about the cabin for some place to discard it. Wow. That seems impossibly long ago and also impossibly ridiculous. Here I am, standing on a continent of plastic garbage, and here I was all worried about the proper way to dispose of something barely bigger than a thread.

Despite their newness, their freshness, the shorts seem to want to meld into the garbage, the cells to become a part of the Petri dish, to disappear into it.

I would have left them, but the sun blazes hot and I didn't put sunscreen on any skin that was covered by clothing if you know what I mean and I think you do, so I pull the shorts up from their cozy nest and put my legs through, one at a time, going commando. I think about stuffing the wad of underwear into my pocket—the right pocket. Another trick I'd learned. Clean on the left, soiled on the right. That way you don't accidentally blow your nose with poop. Or wipe your butt with snot. But the turd is goopy and I don't want to risk it leaking out.

I look down. Next to my foot is a magazine, open to an ad I'd actually taken the product shot for. A plastic bin. A thing to hold your things, I was thinking when the layout came in. I rip the pages out of the magazine and wrap it around my underwear wad. Now it's a thing to hold the thing that used to hold my thing, I think, but now it's holding the thing that came out of my other thing.

Should I cover the hole? Boy Scouts say yes. But Boy Scouts hike and camp on dirt. I decide that the idea of covering up a hole is to keep excrement from getting into the paws or mouths of unsuspecting creatures, and now I feel terrible for having made a hole all the way down to the water.

"You'll know for next time," I tell myself. "And maybe the fish will forgive me."

"Why wouldn't they?" I answer. "They shit in the water, too."

I pick my way back to my ersatz campsite and carefully place the magazine pages holding my soiled underwear alongside the rest of my stuff. How meaningful. Putting my shit with the rest of my shit.

Whatever.

I think about rooting through my duffel bag and putting on a new pair of underwear, but why? It's warm and I feel unencumbered. Free.

I LOOK INLAND. Funny word, inland, when you're not exactly on land, but what else would you call it? It does look like land, though.

The garbage rises in a slope from the beach, gradually at first, and then steeply to a peak like a volcano. A wisp of a cloud near the peak accentuates the effect.

I'm overcome by a desire to see what's up there. Not that I don't already know. It's garbage. More garbage. Just higher up above the water. But it's Everest to my Sir Edmund Hillary; it's there.

But what about my stuff? Should I leave it? I can't carry it all. Besides, it's not like anyone's going to come here looking for stuff to steal. Nobody wants garbage. That's why this place is even here.

When I was just getting started, living in New York. The garbage collectors had gone on strike and bags of trash were piling up on every curb. I passed my neighbor Rudy coming down the stairs, carrying a huge gift-wrapped box. Up until that day, Rudy and I had never exchanged more than a hello in the stairwell, but this day, Rudy was so cheerful. "You know what this is?" he asked.

"Looks like a present," I answered.

"Exactly!" Rudy was beaming.

"You going to a party?"

"Better. I'm taking out the trash."

I must have looked confused, so Rudy elaborated. "I'm sick of all the trash piling up in my apartment, so I put it all in a box, wrapped it up real pretty, and I'm going to leave it on the curb."

I had to admit that the idea was brilliant. Thing is, it isn't until just now, as I look up the slope of the giant volcano of garbage, that I realize. Isn't that what I do for a living? Wrap up garbage real pretty so that somebody will want it?

I look over my stuff. The only thing that distinguishes it from all the other detritus that makes up the not-land mass is the way it's arranged in an organized manner. So I knock over cases, place one duffel bag askew from the others, hide the case of water and the nicer-looking cases under old mattresses and crates. When I'm done, it's hard for even me to tell what's worth keeping and what might have been thrown away.

And that raises an obvious question. What really is worth keeping, at least in the immediate future, as I go off to explore?

The camera, obviously. A bottle of water. What about the satellite phone? Yes. A jacket? Nah. But the knife, the one Ansel had left for me? Definitely. What about the flare gun? Should I bring it?

Why?

Flare guns are for signaling for help. And I'm pretty much at the place where there wouldn't be any help, no matter how badly I might need it.

I leave it with the rest of the stuff.

I start off, then stop. Now that my valuable stuff is indistinguishable from garbage, how will I ever find it again?

About twenty paces away, I see the mast of a sailboat lying

on top of a mass of white plastic sheeting. That'll do. Not too far from the mast, a forty-gallon drum is sunk halfway into the surface, its open end toward the sky. Perfect. I use Ansel's knife to cut a rectangle of the white plastic, poke holes through two of its corners, and then tie it to the top of the mast with some of the fishing line.

A flag. A white flag.

The flag is sad, plain. But it could be so much more. It could be the flag of a country.

Couldn't it?

Like Hernán Cortés, who planted the flag of Spain and claimed the lands of Central America, what's to say I can't do the same thing? Nothing, actually. This land isn't even land. It belongs to no one.

Or wait. It belongs to me. Doesn't it? Couldn't it?

My head races with possibilities. This could be my own sovereign country.

What else do countries do?

Well, they tax their citizens. They make treaties with other countries. They codify laws and mete out justice. They exploit natural resources and labor to provide strategic and/or financial advantage for the ruling class. They encourage tourism. They wage war.

This could be a country, couldn't it? My country. If the Chinese could basically dump landfill into the Bay of China to create islands that expand their borders, why couldn't a congealed mass of garbage have a flag, a national anthem, and an army?

I want to decorate the flag, I really do, to make it look less like surrender. But the point is exactly not to have it draw attention to itself.

I place the mast into the drum. It leans at an angle and I figure that's probably a good thing, too, so I shove more of the white plastic sheeting into the drum to keep the mast stable. If anyone comes by, it'll look as if someone might have just been messing around with the trash. And even if someone comes to investigate the flag, they'd have to be pretty lucky to stumble across my things—the valuable things.

The only flaw is that I'm relying on the bad luck of others to keep me from losing my stuff. Really, if anybody happens by, and then sees the flag, and then decides to take a closer look, their bad luck already isn't exactly working in my favor. But what else can I do?

As I pick my way uphill, toward the slope of what looks like a volcano, preparing to climb with a camera slung around my neck, PowerBars and a knife in my pockets, a bottle of water and a satellite phone in my hands, I'm thinking it's interesting how I had to winnow down all the garbage I brought to the island of garbage to only the absolutely necessary garbage I planned to take on a hike.

Whatever.

When I'm 200 yards or so away, I turn back. I can make out the mast, the flag hanging limp in the breezeless air, but even from this short distance it doesn't exactly stand out. I'm only just beginning my ascent. How am I going to be sure to find my way back?

I'll deal with that later. Right now, what I want to deal with is the whole country thing. I start to climb.

If I'm going to have a country, my country has to have a name. The Pacific Garbage Patch, while honest, isn't exactly the kind of name you put on a tourist brochure.

Remember pilchards? Yeah, no. Nobody ordered pilchards until they changed the name to Cornish sardines. After that, they were the trendiest fish on the menu, lovely grilled with a crisp pinot gris. I know about pilchards firsthand, since I was the guy they hired to photograph the little bastards for the in-store part of the rebranding in the UK market.

So. The Pacific Garbage Patch is a total no-go.

Problem is, I suck at naming.

When I was eight, my mom said I could get a dog.

What happened was, I came home from school one day to find the back door wide open. I didn't think much of it and did what I always did: got myself a Pop-Tart and a glass of milk from the kitchen and parked myself on the floor in front of the TV.

Only there was no TV.

When my mom got home later that afternoon after work, there I was, lying on my stomach on the floor in the empty living room, drawing in a coloring book.

Mom bustled about the house in a panic, totting up the things that had been taken: the stereo, her jewelry, the collection of Lladró figurines, her grandmother's silver. I never felt like I was in any sort of danger and the missing TV was really only a minor inconvenience. I left it on all afternoon while I waited for Mom and Dad to get home, but I didn't really pay much attention to the reruns of *I Dream of Jeannie* or *The Munsters*. Mostly I colored in my coloring books, doing my best to make the images as realistic as possible. Although I did like the commercials. It's funny, now that I think about it, how I dismissed the shows as being unrealistic but thought the commercials presented nothing but the truth. And not just the truth, but a perfected form of truth.

When Mom came in, I was concentrating really hard on an intricate section of the thing I was coloring, so much that I was only vaguely aware that Mom's voice added sound to what had been an unusually quiet afternoon. Until she declared that we were getting a dog.

That got my attention.

I was so excited I spent the next three days trying to come up with the perfect dog name. I talked about it relentlessly, trying out names, discarding ones that didn't capture the dogness of the dog I wanted to have. Finally, after boring and annoying Mom incessantly, I announced that I had come to a decision. I was going to name the dog, my dog... Dog.

I never got the dog.

It wasn't like Mom ever took back the promise, but it just became less and less critical. The insurance company was generous in paying off the claim, and before you knew it, we had a new, better TV and stereo. The Lladró figurines didn't get replaced, but the hutch that had held them started to be filled with collectibles from the Franklin Mint, plates and spoons the family never ate with and which I was told were not for me to play with under any circumstances.

There's a lesson. A thing's value can be expressed as the inverse proportion of its utility.

Grace?

Whatever.

I hinted about the dog once in a while, but Mom put me off with "Can we talk about this later?" and "Didn't I just buy you a brand new TV?" After a while I let it go. It was a betrayal, but really, nothing I wasn't already used to. And rather than do anything about it, I decided that when I was a grown up, I'd get my own dog.

Which I never did.

And I guess that makes me just like my mom.

Sometimes, when I think about that whole naming thing, I wonder if maybe I was simply being too literal.

But I like being literal. I find comfort in knowing clearly what a thing is. Maybe it has something to do with this deficiency I feel I have, this inability to evaluate things.

The problem with deficiencies like this, though, is that you can't possibly know what characteristic or skill or talent you don't have. It's like, can people who can't carry a tune tell that they're singing off-key?

That's probably what drew me to photography, though. That suspicion that there's this thing that I can't do, that I can't quite understand things the way they are. I mean, what's more literal than photography? By definition, it's the literal representation of something.

Okay, it's more. Or can be. Photography, at least in my

hands, is more than the literal representation; it's the idealized representation of something. Its best angle, in the best light, at the most flattering focal length. It may be a subtle distinction, but it's an important one. Anybody can snap a photo, but it takes an artist's eye and a craftsman's training to create a photograph.

Which brings me back to this country thing. Maybe instead of the Pacific Garbage Patch, it could be the Great Pacific Garbage Patch. Great makes it sound, well, great.

Or not. If I'd decided to name my dog Great Dog, would Mom have kept her promise?

No. Not even if the dog was a Great Dane.

True story: One of my early location assignments, my first boondoggle. The ad agency hired me to fly to somewhere in Saskatchewan to photograph fields of rapeseed. That's what it was called. Rapeseed. Like who thinks that's a good name? Canadian farmers, it turned out. New York ad execs, on the other hand, seemed to think there was something a tad problematic with selling an oil that had the word "rape" in it and eventually, an oily group of them managed to convince the farmers that they could make more money if they paid the ad agency a hefty sum to come up with a newer, better name.

It wasn't until I'd delivered the shots that someone told me what they were actually doing. They were rebranding rapeseed. It was going to be called Canola. The word came from "Canada" with "Low Acid" added to the end. Kind of dumb, but better than rapeseed.

That. That's what a couple dozen million bucks gets you.

That's not to say it wasn't money well spent. Canola oil became a thing and the farmers made back their investment easily, but I couldn't help but wonder if a better name might have done them even more good.

And then I wonder why you would even bother.

Perfect is the enemy of good, Dad used to say. I don't know why he said it, given that he never seemed to pursue either good or perfect, but I came to understand what the saying meant. So what if the name Canola was mediocre? Any name would be better than rapeseed, except maybe shitgrain or makesyouretch-weed.

So what am I going to name the Pacific Garbage Patch? Grpagarpa? Like what they did with Canola?

Ugh.

What's better, if only a little better? Better enough to put on a flag on one of those little plaques that the delegates to the UN have in front of them while they debate the latest atrocity?

Turns out, it's not as easy to name a new country as you'd think. Niger and Nigeria? I don't know which one was there first, but seriously? It's almost like the people from the new one said, "Oh yeah?" Like someone started a soda company called Koka-Cola. Or a car rental company called Hurts.

People from Nigeria are called Nigerian, but people from Niger are called what? Turns out, they're called Nigerien. For real. I don't know how I know that.

So Virginia is out of the question.

Patagonia? That's a nice name—comes with some really positive connotations, but yeah, it's already part of another country. Not that it really matters. Georgia, for example. They named a republic Georgia. After a shitty state where white people try to do everything they can to keep Black people from getting all uppity and voting.

Problem is, Patagonia isn't just a country. It's also a clothing brand.

Then again, maybe that's a good thing. Patagonia the company could sponsor Patagonia the country. That might be a really good fit, actually.

Like that would actually happen.

Nah, the name needs to be something that only vaguely connotes something. Like... Elsmere. Only without the British sound. Elsmero. Elsmeridad. Nah. Those sound like something out of *Romancing the Stone 4*.

This is hard.

The real problem is the word Garbage. Pacific is fine. And even Patch, that doesn't bring it down all that much, even though it makes the place sound small. Like Lesser Antilles. But Garbage, there's where you get hung up.

Thing is, it's garbage, this mini continent. But so what? Does the name have to be truthful? Everybody knows that Greenland is icy and Iceland is green. When I saw the Rio Grande that one time, it wasn't all that grande.

Maybe it could be named after the people—person—who make up its population. If Scotland is the land of the Scotts, maybe this could be Alexland?

Is England the land of the Engs? I've never met anybody named Eng. Or Ire, come to think about it. But I do know two guys named Scott. Three, if you count Scott Markham, the guy who used to be my landlord.

Hey, maybe it could be New something. Like New York or New Zealand. I could name it after someplace I like. I like New Mexico. Is New New Mexico too weird?

Maybe I could combine a couple of different things. New Great Britain. Lesser New Great Britain. North Lesser New Great Britain.

One thing is for sure: you want to make sure that whatever the name is, it's something you can fit into a national anthem. The United States of America is a perfect example of a failure there. The name doesn't even try to fit.

Then again, do they ever say "France" in "La Marseillaise"? Isn't the song actually about Marseilles?

What about "Hatikvah"? "The March of the Volunteers"? "God Save the Queen"?

The Canadian one, though. That one goes, "Oh Canada," so yeah, that one has the name of the country in it.

It would be cool to have someone famous come up with an anthem. Like Alanis Morissette. I met her at a party once.

She seemed nice. Okay, I didn't entirely meet her. I got a drink, though, just as she was walking away from the bar. I said hi, the way you do to celebrities, pretending like you know them in hopes that they won't realize they don't know you and they'll compensate by engaging you in conversation. It didn't work with Alanis Morissette, though. She just smiled and continued on her way. But still, isn't she friends with Evan and Nadine?

Oh right.

Doesn't matter. She'd be a lousy one to write an anthem anyway. Who needs an anthem that's all angry and bitter?

You know who'd be great, though? Lyle Lovett. I met him once, too. It was in Costa Rica, when I was hired to shoot that coffee plantation—the one it turned out was growing more marijuana than coffee. I took a weekend on the back end and flew out to Manuel Antonio—the most beautiful beach I've ever seen. I needed to be back in the States to deliver the film by Monday and the Sunday puddle jumper flight back to San José had been canceled. I got the last ticket on the Monday flight, and standing on the grass next to the little dirt airstrip in the heat, waiting for the tiny plane to taxi over, a tall, skinny American guy with black eyes and a pompadour staggered over, a perky twenty-something Victoria's Secret model draped off of his arm, and asked all the passengers if they'd sell him their tickets. All of the rest of them said no. They were students and had to be back in class in San José that afternoon, so the guy turned to me, demanding that I give up my seat. When I said I couldn't, the guy got mean. "Do you even know who I am?" he asked. I did, or I'm pretty sure I did anyway, but I pretended I didn't and also pretended that it didn't matter. Which, sadly, it did. I always liked Lyle Lovett's music, but if I didn't deliver the negatives by Monday, I'd probably never work again.

I wanted to apologize even then, but I knew that if I did, I'd end up relenting and letting him have my ticket, not even taking his money for it, so I turned and walked into the meager shade of the palm tree that the students were huddled under while Lyle Lovett—if it was Lyle Lovett—cursed up a storm. The students, apparently taking Lyle Lovett's side, even though they wouldn't give up their own seats, gave me the cold shoulder, indignant that I wouldn't help out a millionaire who just spent the weekend getting laid by a model, and as noisy as the flight was, it felt painfully silent. And once again, I'm sitting there wondering just how I ended up being the bad guy.

Maybe this could be a way to make it up to him: "Hey, Lyle. Remember that time when you couldn't get on the flight back to San José from Quepos because nobody would give up their seat? Well, sorry about that, but I have a really cool idea for you."

Yeah, right. That kind of shit only happens in the movies.

All the talking amongst myself distracts me so much that I don't even notice I've reached the top until I crest the summit. From down by the water, the peak looked kind of pointy, but from up here it's pretty flat. Wasn't expecting that. Flat and actually kind of big.

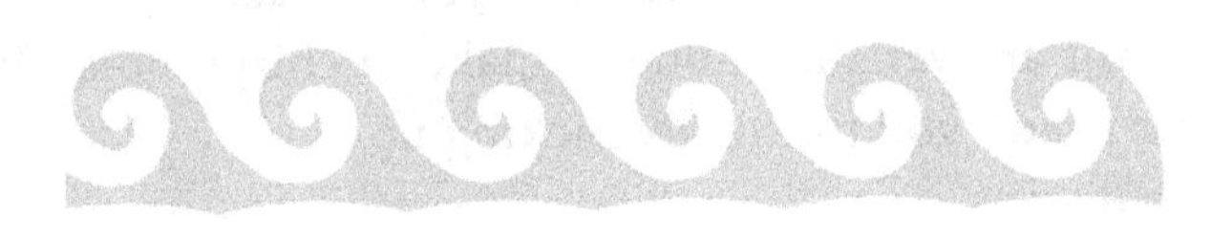

I'M WINDED FROM the climb, so I sit down on the carcass of a stainless steel fridge, lying on its side, and stare out at the garbage stretching down and out below me to the blue blue water.

Down and out.

It's quiet up here, but I can still hear the water, the constant shhhhhh, shhhhhh, shhhhhh as it laps at the shore.

The refrigerator I'm sitting on is a Hotpoint, a model that I'd photographed for a catalog. Not that long ago, either, which means that this fridge is pretty new.

At the time, I asked Fran about it. Hotpoint. Who names a refrigerator Hotpoint? She was blasé. "Doesn't matter, Doll," she told me, "as long as the check clears."

So maybe the name doesn't make a difference. Probably not. Whoever bought this one probably replaced it with the next year's model. The one I didn't get to shoot because at lunch, I made the mistake of asking the client the same question I asked Fran. The rest of the afternoon was chilly—chilly in a way no refrigerator could cool a studio.

And suddenly there's this braying sound, like I'd set off

some kind of an alarm. What would be making that kind of noise out here in the middle of the ocean? The satellite phone, it turns out.

I didn't know satellite phones could actually receive calls. But if it can, that means it has a phone number. I wonder what it is. Whoever's calling knows it. Maybe I'll ask.

When I answer the phone, it makes a chirpy noise, like a sarcastic thank you for finally picking up.

It's Grace.

"I know you're probably busy, so I won't keep you," she starts. No hello. No how are you? No I'm glad to hear your voice. She won't keep me. But she'll call when she wants something.

"What's up?" I reply, trying not to sound as depressed as I feel. Like she'd notice.

"You know how my car makes that funny noise? Well now it's making a different one and I need to get a new one, only the dealership says you need to approve the purchase."

"Did you water the ficus?" I ask.

"What?"

"The ficus. In the living room."

"Why are you asking me about the ficus?"

"Because it needs to be watered. Every day."

She doesn't answer. Instead, a man's voice comes on. She must have handed the phone to the salesman.

"Mr. Jamieson, it's Bob Frank at Bob Frank BMW." Not just the salesman. The owner. Of course. "If you could just give me your—" I press my finger against the button that hangs up the phone. Crap. Forgot to ask what the number was. When I give it long enough to be sure that when I take my finger off, the call is disconnected, I let go. I dial Kathryn.

"I hear you're king of your own domain," she says.

"Yeah, I started an offshore tax haven," I joke back, hoping she doesn't ask me what it's called.

"Hmmm... You know that doesn't do you any good without income, right? What's up?"

"I want to double-check who has access to my accounts," I tell her. "And I should probably update my will."

"You're going to need a notary for that."

Gunfire. Sounds like gunfire, anyway. Two shots, Bap-Bap!, just like that.

"Hold on a sec," I say, putting my hand over the mouthpiece. I look around to see where it might be coming from, but I don't see anything, anyone. Maybe I'm imagining. But how? There's nothing there, nobody. Even the water is hundreds of yards away and below.

"See anything?" I ask myself.

"No. You?"

"Did you just ask yourself if you saw something after you just told yourself you didn't?" Sometimes, talking to yourself doesn't make a lot of sense.

I'm no expert on gunfire. I've never covered a war or an insurrection. I'm not that kind of a photographer. I only do boring stuff: product shots, tabletop, sometimes unremarkable location stuff. But there was that one time in Ecuador when I was supposed to be photographing a banana plantation outside Guayaquil. I was staying in Cuenca, waiting for whoever needed to decide to decide that the bananas were ready to be photographed, and a day delay turned into a week, which turned into two weeks, so I spent my days wandering the city.

This one day, I stumbled onto a demonstration, just rounded the corner and there I was, out in the middle of this no-man's land, this DMZ, a line of students blocking the entire road to the left, holding signs and marching aggressively toward a line of cops in riot gear marching aggressively back at them from the right. Both lines suddenly stopped when they saw me. Stopped and fell silent.

I backed up, back around the corner. And as soon as I was clear, I could hear the tension ratchet up again, and even though I didn't see any of it, I heard what sounded like gunfire. Like what I heard just now. Only here, now, it isn't accompanied by wails and shouts and a cacophony of tromping feet.

I ran away down the street I'd come down, ran as fast as I could, but I was overtaken by several students who ran faster, one of them gripping his upper arm, which was bleeding profusely.

It wasn't until I got back to the hotel that I realized I'd been carrying my camera and that it hadn't occurred to me to take a single photo. I felt ashamed at that, like I was some kind of fraud, and didn't leave the hotel again until I got a call from the art director that the shoot had been called off.

I never said a word to anyone about the incident, but it haunts me.

Every time I think of that, I think of the first morning of the photo workshop. I was up way before dawn and I wandered out in front of the old farmhouse they had us staying in. Must have been jet lag that had me up at 4:00. Must have been jet lag that had Janusz up, too. I found him leaning against a wall, smoking a cigarette, his camera perched on a rock. No tripod.

It was a misty morning and the sun wasn't up yet. I wandered over and it was easy enough to see that with the 16, Janusz had framed up most of the farmhouse wall, with room at what was then a nondescript gray sky. Maybe it was a nice composition. From where I was standing, I couldn't see anything that would make a shot like this particularly special.

"Birds," Janusz said by way of explanation.

"Birds?"

"They come out when sun hits wall."

We were on the west side of the farmhouse. So from the side we were on, you'd never see it. Surely Janusz knew that.

Janusz must have seen the question mark on my face.

"Light and composition, they are easy," he said. "Moment is hard."

I nodded as if I understood, but I didn't. And Janusz hadn't said that thing yet, the thing about light she travel in a straight line, so I had no idea how profound this guy could be. And then he explained, "You must arrive at moment before the moment arrive at you..."

That day in Cuenca, that was the day I got what he was talking about. I had utterly failed to arrive at the moment before the moment arrived at me.

That night, when we all gathered for the first time since we'd met back in the States, Janusz showed us the shot. The composition was better than I expected. But the light! It didn't hit the wall, of course, but what it did hit was a swirl of swallows taking flight, gilding their feathers as they headed toward the sky.

Composition, light, moment.

I remember the phone in my hand, place the receiver to my ear, but Kathryn is gone.

Whatever.

I MAKE A MENTAL INVENTORY of all the photographs I've taken. Not the work-related ones—the ones I got paid for—but all the ones I think are good as photographs. They're all composed well and every single one of them has, if I say so myself, extraordinary light, but of them, of the dozens I'm proud of, I can only think of five or six in which I managed to capture a crucial moment. Where I arrived at the moment before the moment arrived at me.

The sound of a helicopter explodes into the silence, but I'm searching the blue blue sky and can't see it. And then I hear seals. Seals barking. I can't see them, either; the water is too far away, but their barking carries all the way to me, even over the sound of the helicopter's rotors.

And then there it is, as close as it should be, given how loud it is, like it was preceded by its sound. Heralded.

The helicopter is landing. On the garbage.

When it touches down, a man with a vinyl briefcase steps out, wearing an equally cheap suit with his tie undone. He looks improbable as the kind of person who would step out of a helicopter, much less one that's creating a deep impression in the plastic crust that makes up... Crap. The place still doesn't have a name. The guy walks over to me while the pilot, wearing mirrored aviator sunglasses, sits behind the controls, waiting patiently.

When the man gets to me, he thrusts out his hand. "Mr. Jamieson?" he asks. Like he's coming up to a stranger in the busy lobby of a hotel. Like maybe there's someone else here who would answer to Mr. Jamieson. I reach out because that's what you do, shake the man's hand. The man hasn't removed his lit cigarette from between the forefingers of the hand he's shaking my hand with. I nod in assent to the question.

"I'm Edward. Notary." The man removes his hand from mine, places the cigarette back in his mouth, and then uses the same hand to reach into his pocket and produce a business card. When he exhales, the acrid smoke finds its way to my nostrils. The man doesn't notice or doesn't care.

I take the card, look it over. Eadweard. Spelled just like that.

"Ead-weird?" I say and immediately wince. The man just told me how it's pronounced, and here I go, doing exactly what was probably done to him since he was like seven. Eadweard doesn't react.

"Notary?" It says that on the card, too, but I'm at a loss for how to get out of the stale insult I conjured.

"Ms. Milton said you wanted to update your will."

"I guess I did," I say, wondering what this is going to cost. And then wondering why I'd bothered to charter a yacht from Hawaii. "Typical," I say to myself. "If there's a simpler way to do something, I'll find it."

"But only after you exhaust all the harder ways," I tell myself back.

Eadweard opens the briefcase and extracts a single sheet of paper. He hands it to me. It's a will, alright. Says so right there at the top. Will. Last Will And Testament.

"Did Kathryn write up a new will for me?" I ask.

"No. This is your old will. You make whatever corrections

you want, initial them, and I'll notarize the changes."

"Oh." Sure enough, there's my signature down at the bottom.

Sounds simple enough. And it is. With no kids and no siblings, everything goes to Grace. But then there's the problem. If everything doesn't go to Grace, who does it go to?

Eadweard glances at his cheap watch, impatient.

"Um, I need to give this a little thought," I tell him.

"I was under the impression you had determined what changes you wanted to make."

"No, not entirely. Look, can you leave this with me? Maybe come back in a little while?"

Eadweard looks at his watch again, this time not making any effort to conceal the action. "I'm afraid not." He reaches into his pocket, the same one that held the business card, and pulls out a pen. He holds it out for me. A Parker. I shot a lovely catalog for Parker. This very pen, as a matter of fact. It's always fun to see how the circle gets completed, how the persuasive message actually ends up persuading.

I take the pen, use it to point at the words on the page as I read through them. There isn't a whole lot to it when you take out the heretofores and thereins, the legal language.

"This is..." Eadweard starts, taking in the soda bottles, sheets of plastic, discarded refrigerators, and tires that stretch all the way to the horizon.

"It doesn't have a name yet."

"Ah." There's so much in that syllable. Not just judgment, but disappointment. Sadness. I figure Eadweard has kids. Kids who are in their teens and spend most of their time in the basement. Kids who play video games instead of studying or looking for work. Kids who have to have the shit that I help peddle. I know that all from one syllable.

The thought doesn't make me feel any better.

"If you have any ideas for what to call it," I say, turning to gesture toward the island that stretches out below and away, like maybe that could provide some inspiration. When I turn back, the helicopter is taking off, Eadweard next to the pilot, checking his watch once again. I look down to see the will, still in my hand, still uncorrected. I let it go and it floats to the ground. Not ground. Trash. It ends up on top of a pile of those disposable rubber shoes, the knock-off Crocs I shot for those investors in Hong Kong. After the helicopter is gone, the smell of Eadweard's cigarette still lingers.

NOW THAT THE HELICOPTER is gone, I see something where it had been, something pink. An armchair.

Ernie?

Could it be Ernie the chair?

It has to be Ernie the chair. It isn't possible that there are two armchairs like that, pink with gold starbursts.

But then what is possible? Did Grace manage to get rid of Ernie the chair? Did she dump him in the dumpster, which got emptied onto a ship, which what? Spilled its cargo of detritus? Did Ernie the chair float on the open ocean until he and all the other trash congealed into this island?

Impossible. For one thing, Grace would never have carried an armchair to the dumpster. Not in her slippers.

But there he is, on the very summit, a throne. A crown.

I walk over to Ernie the chair and sit, legs across one arm, back against the other, the way I always do, the only way I can. I look out at the wide expanse, garbage stretching away in every direction to a thin ribbon of blue water off toward the even bluer horizon. Even though I'm high up, the view seems unremarkable, and I remember another something Janusz explained during that summer workshop. "View *of* is more exciting than view *from*," I quote Janusz to myself, doing my best to replicate his accent.

"You know that," I answer.

"I know. I forgot."

"Obviously."

Janusz shared that precious nugget one day when we'd come across a little promontory in the middle of a field somewhere near Frassine. Too small to support a village, it was really just a big rock rising out of the plain. The vans stopped a couple hundred feet away and all the students scrambled across the field and started to climb. Except me. I'd twisted my ankle back in Montalcino, and while I could still get around just fine, I didn't feel like pushing it, not unless I knew it would be worth the effort. As I leaned against the van, waiting for all the others to ascend, Janusz came around and joined me. The two of us leaned against the fender, like old friends, it felt like, watching our kids go off on an adventure. Janusz was easily sixty, but built like a mountain goat, with more energy than any of the students. He'd shot for *National Geographic* in sixty-seven countries, so he maybe knew his shit. Still, he was every bit as excited as the students to be shooting in Tuscany, and that's why I was surprised to see him next to the van instead of leading the charge up the hill.

"Not going to climb?" I asked as Janusz lit a cigarette.

That's when Janusz imparted the sage words. "You know what?" he said. "View *of* is more exciting than view *from*." When he said the words, it suddenly made sense. The Eiffel Tower? What's it look like from the top? Who cares? Does anybody ever take a picture of Cape Town from the top of Table Mountain?

Interesting side note: Three years after we did the workshop, Janusz held a multiple-city exhibition to much critical acclaim. The exhibition was titled *Shooting Back* and was exactly that: photos taken from the thing or place that was universally the object of people's interest. The exhibition received millions of dollars in free publicity when he climbed over the velvet ropes and was arrested for taking a photo of all the tourists in the Louvre from the point of view of the *Mona Lisa.*

Whatever.

Later that night, the truth was borne out. All the other students had taken photos from the summit, but not one of the photos was interesting at all. Janusz, on the other hand, had snapped a lovely, compelling composition of seven of the photography students scrambling up the thing.

View *of* is more exciting than view *from.*

And here I am, victim of the same impulse as the students in the workshop, having to find out what you can see from the summit, when the summit is the thing worth seeing.

I take a sip from the water bottle, then put it down on the back of a big-screen television set next to me. The screen isn't level and the bottle slides to the edge, then falls over. It tumbles along the surface of the summit, bouncing off of a Keurig coffee maker and then cascading over the lip and down, bouncing and bounding, splashing water all the way, finally coming to an unspectacular stop several hundred feet below.

Well, there you go, I think. And then I understand that yes, there I do go. Here I sit, on a mountain of garbage I'd claimed as my own. A mountain I'd done more than my part to create. Nobody wants it. Nobody except me. Like having it is something.

"Is it? Is it better to have a mountain of garbage than nothing?" I ask myself.

I don't answer.

And then the sun breaks through. I didn't even notice the clouds, but there must have been clouds because now the sun lights up the expanse below, and suddenly it looks like one of those compositions, like one of those quintessential images of Yosemite. A full tonal range, almost monochromatic, but exactly exactly exactly the way it's meant to be. The light is intense, glaring.

"Find the light, and the image will give herself to you," I say to myself, imitating Janusz's voice. And there it is. The light. The light that is falling on the exquisite composition in front of me. The light that is falling on me.

I am illuminated.

"You are illuminated. And so you reflect," I imitate back. Do I reach for my camera? No. No, I don't. Instead, I reply back to myself. "See what is! Not what you hope!" I say.

"Pattern you don't interrupt is shit."

Pattern you don't interrupt is shit.

This makes me wonder. I wonder whether Janusz was talking about photography. I mean, yeah, he was, but could his little lessons be something... I don't know... bigger?

From where I sit, I can see a lone pelican gliding along the crest of a small wave breaking just off shore, not flapping, its outstretched wings twitching to correct its course, left and right, to stay just inside the curve of the wave.

As I watch the pelican slide past a tiny peninsula of garbage, a dolphin leaps from the water and, before the huge bird can flap out of reach, clamps its mouth around the pelican's foot. The dolphin crashes back into the water, taking the struggling pelican to the depths with it.

Then the water becomes calm again.

And then a fucking annoying bird goes off, somewhere nearby, spewing its desperate sales pitch.

Whatever.

I close my eyes, clench them shut as tight as I can.

I hate the light.

#

About Atmosphere Press

Founded in 2015, Atmosphere Press was built on the principles of Honesty, Transparency, Professionalism, Kindness, and Making Your Book Awesome. As an ethical and author-friendly hybrid press, we stay true to that founding mission today.

If you're a reader, enter our giveaway for a free book here:

SCAN TO ENTER
BOOK GIVEAWAY

If you're a writer, submit your manuscript for consideration here:

SCAN TO SUBMIT
MANUSCRIPT

And always feel free to visit Atmosphere Press and our authors online at atmospherepress.com. See you there soon!

About the Author

Brian Belefant used to be good-looking, but now he has a dog, and not just any dog, but a friendly, goofball dog who loves everybody except Santa Claus.

His short stories appear in *American Writers Review*, *Magpie Messenger*, *Story Unlikely*, *Libretto*, and *Half and One*. He's currently at work on his second novel.

Brian is also an award-winning fine art photographer.

Want to keep up with what he's doing? Scan the QR code or visit belefant.com.

About the Author

Printed in the USA
CPSIA information can be obtained
at www.ICGtesting.com
LVHW042121270824
789273LV00005B/153